D1110431

The Adirondack Kids® #6

Secret of the Skeleton Key

The Adirondack Kids® #6

Secret of the Skeleton Key

by Justin & Gary VanRiper
Illustrations by Carol VanRiper

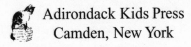

Adirondack Kids Press
Camden, New York

The Adirondack Kids® #6
Secret of the Skeleton Key

Justin & Gary VanRiper
Copyright © 2006. All rights reserved.

First Paperback Edition, March 2006

Cover illustration by Susan Loeffler
Illustrated by Carol McCurn VanRiper

Photograph of pileated woodpecker
© 2004 by Eric Dresser – www.nbnp.com

All rights reserved. No part of this publication may be reproduced, stored in a retrieval system, or transmitted in any form or by any means – electronic, mechanical, photocopying, recording, or otherwise – without prior, written permission of the publisher and copyright owners.

Published by
Adirondack Kids Press
39 Second Street
Camden, New York 13316
www.adirondackkids.com

Printed in the United States of America
by Patterson Printing, Michigan

ISBN 0-9707044-6-1

Other Books
by Justin and Gary VanRiper

The Adirondack Kids®

The Adirondack Kids® #2
Rescue on Bald Mountain

The Adirondack Kids® #3
The Lost Lighthouse

The Adirondack Kids® #4
The Great Train Robbery

The Adirondack Kids® #5
Islands in the Sky

Other Books
by Justin VanRiper

The Adirondack Kids® Story & Coloring Book
Runaway Dax

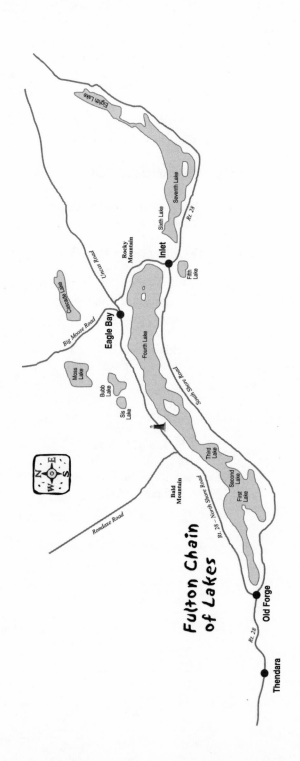

Contents

Jackie drew the arrow back once again. *see page 24*

For Addison Danielle Kelly

second grandchild
second niece
soon to climb the high peaks

Chapter One

The New Kid

"Man overboard!" yelled Justin Robert, as his sailboat collided with another small wooden craft on the silver surface of Fourth Lake.

A sudden breeze had caused his boat to turn sideways without warning in the early morning fog and plow into the side of a helpless vessel moving alongside his own. He threw off his purple bucket hat and plunged headlong into the still, dark water.

"No fair!" cried his friend and neighbor, Nick Barnes, who reached over the end of the dock and plucked his capsized and wounded boat from the contest. He pointed his bruised vessel at Justin who was still in the water retrieving his own small boat. "You snapped my mast and now the sail is all messed up. If you're going to cheat, then I am not playing."

Jackie Salsberry sighed. The Adirondack summer was more than halfway over, and the boys were still acting like...boys. "Will you two stop fighting?" she said, and pointed out along the shoreline. "See? My boat has already made it to the other dock."

1

It was true. Between patches of fog, they could see her small craft had indeed reached the far-away finish line they had all agreed upon. "I win again," she said. "Just like I am going to do in the real race on Saturday."

Justin rescued his own boat from the water and climbed the short ladder to join them back on the dock. He stood facing Jackie, his other lifetime summer friend, and cradled the small craft, still dripping wet, in the palm of his extended hand. He didn't understand how she could even win a race with hardly any wind, but he couldn't let her comments go unchallenged. "Sailing one of these little boats we made at the Blue Mountain Museum will be a lot different from what we'll be sailing this weekend in the **Anything That Floats Race**," he said.

"I don't doubt that," Jackie shot back. "The boat you and Nick plan to sail this weekend won't just tip over, it will sink for sure."

"How do you know?" said Nick. "You haven't even seen our boat yet. And besides, just because you've won a few races, it doesn't mean you know everything about sailing."

Jackie shook her head. "I heard all about the wreck you have hiding in the woods that your uncle towed to your camp last week," she said. "Work on it all you want." She shrugged and spoke with unnerving confidence. "It doesn't matter what you'll be racing in anyway. I have 75 square feet of sail that will carry my 120 pounds of hull ahead of

2

you so fast that, when I look back, your boat will seem like it's anchored. It really won't matter if you sink or not."

Justin didn't quite understand all Jackie had just said about her sail and hull and the square feet and the 120 pounds, but he did know one thing for sure. She fully expected to win. And she had the trophies at her family's Fourth Lake island camp to back her up. Three victories in three years in real sailboat races, even against adults. He glanced past her shoulder and changed the subject. "Hey, look," he said. "It's that new kid."

The new kid was little more than four foot four, and was all tan. As the fog slowly burned off the lake, a slight breeze was picking up. It tossed his sandy-colored hair which was bleached nearly white by the hot August sun. Sounds were exaggerated on the quiet lake this time of day, and it was surprising that motor boats with skiers weren't already out to take advantage of the flat water.

The boy stood in his swim trunks on the dock across from them, waving Jackie's small boat back and forth high up over his head. "Want me to bring it to you?" his voice echoed out to them.

"Do you think someone finally bought the huge camp and boathouse?" said Jackie.

"Hope he didn't mind we used his dock for our finish line," said Nick.

"What do you think, you guys?" asked Justin. "Should we invite him to Pioneer Village?"

"It's fine with me," said Jackie. "What do you think, Nick? You're still the mayor."

Nick struck a pose to give the impression he was in deep thought.

Justin shrugged. "Go ahead and take your time," he said. He picked up his bucket hat and waved it to the new kid, motioning for him to meet them among the thick pine trees along the shore which sheltered their secret village. He and Jackie raced the length of the long plank dock and veered off toward the woods.

"Why did you even bother to ask me?" yelled Nick. His sneakers pounded the dock as he ran after them. "I am the leader. I didn't vote yet. You can't rush the leader..."

Chapter Two

The Robert Louis Stevenson

"So, where's the new kid?" asked Nick, panting for breath. He had finally caught up with Justin and Jackie in the middle of Pioneer Village, their small community of buildings made from branches and sticks where no adults were allowed. "He should have been here easy by now."

Justin looked at his sailing partner. There was a touch of panic in his eyes. "You don't think he found our –"

Nick groaned and was already running on his way to the trail that connected their family camps.

"Stay here, Jackie!" said Justin, and took off after Nick.

The two friends broke from the worn path and pushed through some low pine boughs, only to realize their worst fear. Their boat had been discovered. The new kid was examining the large, crude wooden vessel that was tipped in the direction of the lake and was resting on a narrow track made from stripped logs.

"Hi. I'm Douglas Taylor," the new boy said. "We

just moved into the camp next door." He motioned toward their vessel. "Neat boat."

"We didn't want anybody to see it yet," said Nick.

"We still have a lot of work to do," said Justin.

"I'll say," said Jackie, who had snuck up behind them.

"What are you doing here?" said Justin. "I told you not to follow us."

Jackie ignored them all and walked up to the crude hull of the mystery boat. She began picking at multiple layers of peeling paint, revealing a faded rainbow of colors underneath. "It looks like this boat was painted about 50 times," she said. "Let's see, there's blue and green and red and white –"

"Stop picking at it," said Justin. He pushed her hand down. "You might make some of the caulk come out of the boards and make holes."

"I heard a loud knocking sound in the trees. That's how I found the boat," Douglas explained. "I wasn't sneaking around or anything."

Rat-tat-tat-tat. A small shower of wood splinters descended on the four Adirondack kids. They all looked up and used their hands to shield their eyes from the cascading splinters. A pileated woodpecker was hammering on a decaying tree.

"Yep, that's what I heard," said Douglas.

The bird's long black body blended in with the dark trunk, and its pointed red crest was a blur while it continued to search for insects and an early morning meal.

"How does he keep from knocking his brains out?" wondered Nick aloud.

"You should be worried about your boat sinking," said Jackie. She reached down and picked up several of the long slivers of wood the woodpecker had made, and handed them to Justin. "Here," she said. "Maybe you can use some of these wood chips to start plugging any holes."

"Very funny," said Justin. He liked Jackie a lot, but she was always trying to win every game they ever played. Just once he would like to beat her at something. "Do you always have to be best at everything we do?" he asked.

Douglas looked at her. "I'll bet you can't beat me at archery," he said.

Justin was right. Jackie could never resist a challenge. She faced the new kid squarely, put her hands on her hips and wagged her head at him. "How much do you want to bet?" she said, as she grabbed her small boat from his hand.

Douglas smiled and glanced at the back of the real boat where the letters, R L S, were hand painted in black. He pointed at them. "What does that mean?" he asked.

Jackie looked and laughed. "Is that the name of the boat?" she asked. "Let me guess what the letters stand for." She pretended to be thinking really hard. "I've got it," she said. "Real Loser's Ship." She smiled broadly. "Am I right?"

Douglas tried not to laugh, but couldn't help it.

7

Justin didn't think it was funny at all.

Nick scrambled up onto the deck of the boat and disappeared into the cabin. A moment later he emerged wearing a red bandanna wrapped snugly around his skull. He held a plastic bottle full of soda in one hand and carried a primitive, handmade sword with a wide wooden blade in the other. A black patch covered his left eye.

Using the stern of the boat like a pulpit, he stood and beckoned his friends to gather round as he sang:

"Fifteen men on the dead man's chest
Yo - ho - ho - and a bottle of rum!"

Then he raised his blade and began a short speech in his most annoying pirate voice.

Jackie leaned and, slightly covering her mouth, whispered to Douglas. "Get ready," she said. "Whenever he puts that eye patch on, he talks like this."

"We be sailing this new ship for sure in just a few days," Nick said loudly, out of the side of his mouth. "We be raising sail in search of treasure and to win races." He cleared his throat. "And I, Captain Flint, will tell ye the name of our great vessel." He tapped the stern just above the black letters with his sword. "Just a few days of hard work by me loyal crew, and we will launch her the *Robert Louis Stevenson!*"

As if providing a drum roll for a special event, the pileated woodpecker began another series of resounding blows against the tree above.

8

Nick raised his blade and began a short speech
in his most annoying pirate voice.

"I christen you the *Robert Louis Stevenson!*" Nick bellowed in a mock ceremony. Then he swung the soda bottle high over his head and brought it crashing down hard on the back of the boat.

The bottle exploded on impact and soda jettisoned in every direction, soaking everyone with sticky green liquid.

Everyone groaned, but before any one of them could get their hands on Nick to throw him into the lake, the earth began to shake violently beneath their feet and a sound like a rushing train assaulted their ears.

"What did you do?" Justin cried out to Nick, as he fell to the ground.

"It wasn't me!" yelled Nick, who would never take responsibility for anything that ever went wrong. He began blaming the woodpecker, as he also lost his balance and fell backward onto the deck of the boat.

The woodpecker flew away as the dying tree it was drilling giant holes into snapped in two, the top beginning a deadly descent directly toward Jackie and Douglas below. They scrambled out of the way just as the trunk landed in the very spot where they had been listening to Captain Flint.

The ground continued to vibrate, and a small boulder holding the boat in place came loose and slowly rolled away.

"Help!" cried Nick. In less than a minute, the fierce shaking stopped, but not before the *Robert Louis Stevenson* had been released, carrying its

helpless captain along the slippery log tracks
downward toward Fourth Lake.

Chapter Three

"We're Doomed!"

Justin grabbed the rope ladder and hauled himself up and onto the deck just before the vessel broke completely away. "We'll be shipwrecked before we even sail!" he said, as he tumbled alongside his friend.

Totally unprepared for the launch, the two reluctant sailors scrambled to their knees, and dared to grab and peer over the rail as the boat pushed through a stand of thick pines. Bristling branches tore at the sail and slapped at the hull and their faces as they gained momentum and descended more and more rapidly toward the lake.

"We're headed for a watery grave!" cried Nick, as he still hung onto the rail but lowered his head to avoid the relentless onslaught of smacking tree limbs. "Were doomed!"

Like an untested ride at an amusement park, the boat creaked and rocked as it gained more and more speed. It slid down the bare log tracks through the forest and burst through a final row of trees and out into the open.

The momentum of the boat was enough to carry it over the rocky shoreline where it momentarily became airborne and then crashed bow first into the water. The entire vessel easily cleared the shore, and remained intact as it splashed hard onto the surface, pushing a series of waves in every direction.

As the *Robert Louis Stevenson* bobbed aimlessly a few feet from shore, her stunned captain and crewman slowly stood to survey their situation. For the first time that entire summer, neither friend said anything to each other for at least 60 seconds.

From the direction of Eagle Bay, they could hear the faint sound of a siren.

Then it was Jackie's voice they heard. She stood with Douglas on the shore and called from the rocks. "Are you both okay?"

"We're all right," yelled Justin. He turned to Nick who sat back down to cling to the rail. "Do you still think a woodpecker made this happen?"

Nick shrugged. "What do you think it was?"

"The way the ground shook like that, and then the siren? I think it was an earthquake," said Justin. "Come on. We'd better check out the boat. There's a noise coming from somewhere below the cabin. It might be a leak."

"You'd better go down and check it out," said Nick.

"Why me?" asked Justin.

"Because I'm the captain," said Nick. He scrambled to his feet again and pointed his sword toward his shipmate. "Get thee going or I'll run ye through!"

Before Justin could answer, the source of the noise surfaced. "Dax!" he said. His adopted calico cat and everyday companion appeared on the roof of the cabin. She stretched and yawned.

"She must have been sleeping down there!" said Nick.

Justin picked her up and buried his fingers into the soft, warm bundle of black and rufous and white fur. "I wondered where you were last night, girl," he said.

"A stowaway!" said Nick. "I'll make her walk the plank!"

Justin frowned. "We don't have a plank," he said.

Nick waved his sword. "Well, we are going to be adding one," he said firmly. "For stowaways such as this one." Then, as if warning his friend, he squinted his eyes. "And for traitors!"

"Quiet!" said Justin. "I hear another strange noise – kind of a bumping sound." He put Dax down and leaned over the edge of the boat. The calico jumped up onto the rail next to him.

"What's going on out there?" called Jackie from shore. There was a tone of frustration in her voice. "Is anything wrong?"

Nick held up his hands. "I don't know," he said. "I think Justin found something."

"There's something in the water, banging against the hull," Justin said, and reached out for it. Nick bent on his knees and held firmly to the legs of his friend to prevent him from falling overboard. Justin leaned out even further, and the combined weight of the two boys on the same side of the boat caused it to tip slightly.

"Almost," said Justin. More than half of his body dangled over the edge of the boat. The vessel gently rocked with each movement. Hanging nearly upside down, he began to get dizzy and could feel his face get hot, but he wouldn't give up. "Let me out a little bit more."

Clinging tightly to Justin's legs, Nick began grunting and returned to his role as pirate and captain. "Hurry ye up," he said. "Or I'll just throw ye to the sharks."

"Got it!" Justin said. "Now, haul me back up – or ye lose the prize!"

Chapter Four

Making a Deal

"What was it?" Jackie asked.

"We're not telling," said Nick.

Justin nodded in agreement. "Not even a chance," he said.

The *Robert Louis Stevenson* was safely anchored and roped just offshore between Justin's and Nick's family camps. Before meeting in Pioneer Village at the Rock, he and Nick decided that since everyone had now seen their ship, it didn't matter where they fixed it up.

The two pirates had with them, hidden in a backpack, the secret object they had found in the lake, and saw no reason why they should share their discovery without some extra reward.

"Come on, Justin, tell us," Jackie pleaded.

Justin had never heard Jackie so desperate before. He actually enjoyed the power and tried to change the subject. "My mom said some of the neighbors ran outside in their pajamas after the earthquake hit. I guess they were really scared."

Jackie scowled at him.

"Okay," said Justin. "What will you give us, if we tell you what we found?"

"Yeah," said Nick. "What will you give us?"

Douglas came to Jackie's rescue. "We will let you shoot arrows with us at my camp," he said.

"That's no big deal," said Justin. "We were already going to shoot with you."

"Not if you don't tell us what you found in the lake," said Douglas.

"That's not fair," said Nick. Now it was he who sounded desperate. He looked at his fellow treasure hunter.

Justin liked making Jackie squirm. He thought he would make her wait a little bit longer.

"A bottle," Nick blurted.

"A what?" asked Jackie.

"That's what we found," Nick said. "We found a bottle."

Justin looked at Nick and shook his head. He could not believe his friend had given in so easily. "You're the traitor who is going to walk the plank," he mumbled to his shipmate.

Jackie picked up a pine cone and threw it at Justin. "That's it? You found a dumb bottle? Someone litters in our lake and this excites you?" She stood up to go. "Come on, Douglas, let's go shoot some arrows. It's time for me to beat you."

"Wait," said Justin. "It's nothing like a regular bottle. And that's not all we found." He hesitated for dramatic effect. "We also found something inside the bottle."

17

Jackie sat back down. "Okay, what was inside the bottle?"

"A key," blurted Nick again.

Justin shoved him. "Will you be quiet," he said. "Can't you ever keep any secrets?"

Nick ignored him. "That's right," he said. "We found a skeleton key. And it looks really, really old. It's the kind of key that opens up treasure chests. And we are going to find the treasure, just like in the book, *Treasure Island*." He looked at Douglas. "And then we'll buy our own bows and arrows and we'll buy your giant camp and the boathouse and maybe we will let you come over, and maybe we won't."

"Is that what all this is about?" asked Jackie. "Naming your boat the *Robert Louis Stevenson* and singing, 'fifteen men on a dead man's chest'? You just read *Treasure Island*?"

"What do you know about, *Treasure Island*?" asked Nick. "It's not a girl's book anyway. It's a book just for boys. I've read it two times this summer already. And there's not even one single girl in it!"

"There's not?" said Justin. "Can I borrow it?"

"There is, too, a girl in it," said Jackie.

"There is not," said Nick.

"What about Jim Hawkins' mother," Jackie challenged.

"She doesn't count," argued Nick. "She's not a girl. She's a mom."

"Moms are girls," said Douglas, trying to get in on the conversation.

Jackie looked at Douglas and shook her head. "Don't even bother with Nick – he's impossible," she said. She turned to Justin. "So, let's see the key."

"Yes," said Douglas. "If you want to shoot arrows with us, let us see the skeleton key." He looked at Nick with a fake smile. "You don't own our camp yet!"

Justin sighed and reached into the backpack to retrieve the bottle. It was just as he said. It was different from any bottle they had ever seen. The glass was really thick and tinted aqua in color. He handed it to Jackie.

"Wow, it's really heavy," Jackie said. "And I've never seen a bottle with a round bottom before."

"Maybe that's why it was thrown away," offered Douglas. "Because it was made wrong."

"No way," said Nick, who was an expert on pirates and treasure and ships. "Thick bottles with round bottoms were made to travel on their sides in big boats," he explained. "That way, when the boats rocked out in the waves, the bottles could roll around and even bump into each other and not break."

The glass was hard to see through, so Jackie shook the bottle. It was empty. "So, where's the key?" she asked.

Justin looked puzzled. "Isn't it inside?" He grabbed the bottle back from Jackie and held it up to inspect it. Then he looked at Nick.

"Don't worry, I have it for safekeeping," said Nick, and pulled up his t-shirt.

"You taped the key to your stomach?" said

"I've never seen a bottle with a round bottom before," Jackie said.

Jackie. "Nicholas Barnes, that's disgusting. What is wrong with you?"

"Ouch," said Nick, as he ripped the tape to free the key. Brown from rust, he held up the slender, strange-looking key so they all could see. "We almost found treasure at the beginning of the summer," he said. "I'm not giving up until we find the real thing."

"That bottle and key could have come from anywhere," said Jackie. "It could have floated here through rivers and streams all the way from the ocean."

Nick frowned. "Then we'll sail to the ocean," he said, and began to remove a lace from one of his sneakers.

"What are you doing?" asked Justin.

"The tape is all sweaty and won't stick now," said Nick. "I'm going to tie the key around my neck for safekeeping like the pirates do anyway." He looked at Douglas. "Now can we shoot some arrows?"

Right on Target

"Just because I'm a girl, it doesn't mean I have to go first," said Jackie, as she strapped on an arm guard.

The four Adirondack kids were gathered in an opening near a stand of trees behind the Taylor camp, preparing for an archery contest. A large round target with black, blue and red colored rings was set up 30 yards away from them. In the center of the target was a giant yellow bull's-eye.

"I'll go," said Justin. He was eager to try. He and Nick had made bows from tree branches and string, and one time his dad bought him a plastic bow from a local souvenir shop, but he had never shot a real bow with real arrows before.

Douglas handed Justin the bow, which was almost as tall as he was, and showed him how to stand. Then he helped him place the arrow properly on the bow-string. "Are you ready?" he asked, as he slowly stepped away.

"All set," said Justin.

"Then draw the arrow back and let it fly," said Douglas. "From this distance, try to aim a little low."

Justin drew the arrow back until its yellow feathers nearly brushed his cheek. The further he drew the arrow back, the smaller the target seemed to look. His arms shook a bit and he closed his eyes as he released. The orange shaft flew from his bow.

Smack.

"It's a hit," said Douglas.

Nick cheered, mainly because he was certain he could do better.

Justin opened his eyes. The arrow had hit the target all right. But it was near the outer edge in the black ring. "How many points do I get?" he asked.

"You get three points for getting it in the black ring," said Douglas. "Even if you only hit the white part of the target on the very outside, you still get one point."

Jackie teased Nick. "See, you might still get a point," she said.

"How much for the other rings?" asked Justin.

"It's five points for the blue ring and seven points for the red ring," Douglas explained.

"And how many points for the yellow bull's-eye?" asked Jackie.

Douglas smiled. "I'll tell you after my shot," he said, as he took the bow from Justin. Without hesitation, he reached into the quiver, placed an arrow on the bowstring, drew back and fired.

Smack. Another hit. This one touching the border of the red ring and the yellow bull's-eye.

"You always count the higher color when that

happens," said Douglas. "The yellow bull's-eye is worth nine points, so that's nine points for me. You can't do better than that."

Jackie seemed unimpressed. She took the bow from Douglas and selected another orange arrow from the quiver. She began to draw the arrow back, when it slipped from her hand and fell to the ground at her feet. "Oops," she said, and picked it back up.

Douglas smiled broadly. "That's okay, take your time," he said. "Just do the best you can."

Justin knew what Jackie was doing. So did Nick. But not poor Douglas.

Jackie drew the arrow back once again. This time it soared from her bow with speed and precision.

Smack.

Dead center in the middle of the yellow bull's-eye.

Douglas's smile disappeared and he just stared at the target.

"Next?" asked Jackie, and casually passed the bow to Nick.

"No problem," said Nick, who took the bow eagerly. "I'll just have to split your arrow in half!"

Douglas recovered from the shock of Jackie's perfect shot and turned to Nick. "Let me help you get set," he said.

"No," said Nick, and pulled away. "I don't need any help." While the amateur archer struggled to get his arrow onto the bowstring, Dax appeared in the clearing. She ran to Justin just as Nick prepared to shoot.

24

Nick began a countdown for himself. "Five – four – three – two – one," he said. "Fire."

The arrow sprang from his bow, soared through the air, and disappeared into the woods.

Douglas groaned. "Oh, no," he said. "These are brand new arrows. My mother said if I lost even one, she wouldn't get me any more."

"Can I shoot again?" asked Nick. "That was just a warm-up. It's no fair. Dax made me miss."

"Don't even think about blaming Dax," said Justin. "Why don't you just blame the woodpecker again?"

"Stop arguing," said Jackie. "Let's help Douglas find his arrow."

The three archers followed their new friend into the woods.

And Dax? She was way ahead of them all.

A 15-minute search proved fruitless. They did find some rusty cans, a bent frame from an old lawn chair and a tire rim from a bicycle, but no arrow. They collected the junk and put it all in one small pile. "We'll throw it out later," said Douglas. "First I want to show you something."

He led them to a spot he had discovered while exploring his camp's property earlier in the week. Dax was already there. "What do you think of this big boulder," he said. "It's kind of like the one you meet on at Pioneer Village. I was thinking maybe I could build a town here, too."

Douglas was not exaggerating about the size of the rock. The boulder was big – almost twice the height of Jackie.

"Hey, look, the arrow," said Justin. He bent over and picked it up. "It's broken. Sorry, Douglas, it must have hit the boulder."

Nick grinned nervously and changed the subject. He pointed to a small hole near the base of the giant rock. "Does some animal live down in there?" he asked. "I wouldn't want to build any town with wild animals living in it."

Douglas looked confused. "That hole wasn't there yesterday," he said.

"Get away from there, Dax," said Justin.

The curious calico had inched her way to the dark entrance. She sniffed the ground.

"I mean it, Dax," Justin scolded. "Stay away."

But before he could scoop her up, she hurried into the hole.

Chapter Six

Cave Raiders

"No!" yelled Justin. "Dax, come out of there, right now." Experience had told him shouting at Dax never made her do anything. In fact, she usually did just the opposite of what he wanted her to do, but he had to try anyway.

Nick knelt down, and thrust a long branch into the hole.

"Don't poke her," Justin said.

Nick frowned. "I'm just trying to help," he said, and kept probing with the stick. "The branch isn't even hitting anything. It must be a pretty deep hole."

"Maybe it's a cave," offered Jackie. "If it wasn't here the other day, maybe it was opened up by the earthquake."

"That's true," said Douglas. "There aren't any animal footprints anywhere around it, except Dax's."

"Douglas. Douglas." An adult voice called out from the edge of the woods.

"Sorry I have to leave, you guys. I've got to go get ready for dinner," Douglas said. "My parents are having a big party with a lot of important people. I

"No!" yelled Justin looking down at the hole.
"Dax, come out of there, right now."

28

even have to dress up in a tuxedo. I could ask if you could come."

Nick shivered at the thought of ever having to wear a fancy suit. "I love food," he said. "But I don't think I'd ever dress like a penguin to eat."

Justin wasn't even paying attention. He was totally absorbed with finding Dax, and began making the hole bigger by scooping loose dirt away with his hands.

"That's okay, thanks anyway," Jackie reassured Douglas. "We're going to stay and help Justin."

Justin stopped to catch his breath, which he lost more to panic than to digging. He turned to his friends. "Where's Douglas?" he asked.

"His mom called him to dinner," Jackie said.

"But first he has to dress up like a penguin," said Nick.

Justin looked at Jackie.

Jackie shook her head. "Never mind," she said.

Justin looked back at the hole. It was just barely large enough for him to squeeze his body into. "I'm going in," he said.

"Are you crazy?" said Nick. "You don't know what's in there."

"I know Dax is," Justin said.

"I don't know if that is such a great idea," said Jackie. "What if there's an aftershock?"

Nick looked puzzled. "There can't be any electricity down in that hole," he said. Then he looked up through the forest canopy. "And there's not a lightning cloud in the sky."

"Not that kind of a shock," said Jackie. "You now, an aftershock. It's like a second earthquake in the same spot after a big one." She looked at Justin. "Dax is constantly hiding in kayaks and logs and dark places. She'll come out. She always does."

"I'm not just sitting out here and letting Dax get buried alive," Justin said.

"All right," Jackie said. "But shouldn't we at least get a flashlight?"

Justin looked at the large dark hole that began to look more like a large mouth waiting to devour something. "Well, maybe," he said.

"That's a maybe, and a maybe is yes," said Jackie.

"We have a lot of flashlights at camp," said Nick, happy now to find any excuse to get as far away from the cave as possible.

"You two go and I'll stay here in case Dax comes out," Justin said.

As Jackie and Nick ran toward the Barnes' camp for the flashlights, Justin kept digging. He picked up a larger stone that had a sharp corner. With two hands, he chopped away at the packed earth.

While he worked, he continued to plead. "Dax, come out – I mean it."

Something that wasn't dirt or rock broke loose. Justin picked it up and tried to brush it off. Moist dirt clung to it like glue. The sole of an old boot or shoe. *What is that doing here*? he thought. Several more severe blows with the sharp rock uncovered even more artifacts. He placed each item next to him in a small pile.

Jackie and Nick quickly returned with two flashlights and a head lamp.

Thanks to Justin's steady work, the hole had become a small passageway.

Jackie saw the small pile of debris on the ground next to Justin. She picked up the piece of disintegrating footwear and a broken smoking pipe.

Nick's eyes grew wide. "We are digging in a cemetery, aren't we?"

Jackie slapped his arm with the sole of the shoe. "Don't be ridiculous," she said. "This is all probably part of an old dump."

Justin seized the head lamp. He fastened the straps to his bucket hat and switched on the light. "I'm going in first," he said.

Jackie offered Nick a flashlight. "Do you want to go next?" she asked.

"I don't think so," said Nick. "I'd better wait here in case there's one of those after-shocky things." Jackie stood and stared at him. "Well, somebody would have to run to get help," he said.

"Really?" Justin said. He picked through the small pile of debris he had found and held up a small coin. "I guess all the treasure will be for Jackie and me."

Nick snatched the flashlight from Jackie. "I'll go second," he said.

On hands and knees, each one slowly crawled into the cave.

Chapter Seven

Shivers, Slithers and Slivers

Justin looked back to make sure his two friends were behind him.

"Could you please stop shining that light back in our faces?" Nick complained. "You're making me blinder than a bat."

Jackie agreed. "We're with you," she reassured their leader. "Just keep going straight ahead."

It didn't take long for the three cave raiders to realize they weren't in a cave at all. The first hint was a short set of stone stairs that met them nearly immediately upon entering the hole.

It was awkward to crawl down the slippery and uneven steps. Once fully inside the cavernous space, they realized there was plenty of room to stand up. The walls appeared to be part brick and part solid rock.

"What is this place?" wondered Jackie out loud. It wasn't like her to be so surprised and ask questions. She usually had all the answers, or at least good guesses.

They didn't stand up for long. There were

high-pitched squeaks and a rushing noise suspended in the air somewhere out in front of them, and growing louder by the second. There wasn't even time to point their lights toward the sound. Something in each one of their stomachs told them the same thing, "Fall down!"

What little daylight that poured in through their escape route behind them was suddenly snuffed out as a dark cloud of airborne creatures flew directly over their heads – so many, they temporarily plugged the lighted entrance. With eyes shut tight, the Adirondack kids lay flat on their faces with their hands over the back of their heads and necks until the eerie noise created by a hundred tiny flapping wings had completely passed.

"Bats!" cried Nick, as he cautiously rose again to his feet. He did not know if a sudden shiver he felt was from the aerial assault or the coolness of the underground hallway.

"No kidding," said Jackie. She and Justin also stood up. "I don't get it," she said. "Bats don't go outside in the daylight."

"That's not true," said Justin. "One time we had more than a hundred bats come down our chimney at camp in the middle of the day. They filled the living room and went under the couches and chairs and into the drapes and everywhere. My mom wouldn't sleep there for almost a month!" He shrugged. "Maybe the bats were messed up by the earthquake."

"I vote we get out of here right now," said Nick.

"But what if we start out the hole and the bats try to fly back in here?" said Justin. "Besides, I don't care what you vote for, I'm still going ahead and looking for Dax."

Nick pointed the beam of his flashlight at Jackie, hoping for some support. He was disappointed.

"He's right, Nick," Jackie said, and pushed the light away from her face. "And Dax may never come back this way. I don't know how those bats got in here to begin with, but it wasn't through a hole in the ground that didn't even exist until today. There must be another way in and out of here."

"Unless the earthquake blocked any other way out," said Nick.

That thought made Justin and Jackie hesitate for a moment, but only for a moment. And if the entranceway to the tunnel was a mouth, then Justin led the way deeper into its dark, open throat – step by cautious step. Traveling through the mysterious hallway, only their own shadows appeared in their lights on the brick and stone walls alongside them.

They hadn't walked very far when Justin abruptly stopped. "Oh, no," he said. "It looks like there's nothing ahead but a dead end."

Nick groaned. "Don't say, 'dead'," he said.

"That's not possible," said Jackie. "We never passed by Dax."

Justin moved forward. "Maybe you're right," he said. "It looks like there might be a bend in the tunnel."

There *was* a bend and the three approached it and made the turn.

Far out in front of them appeared to be the frame of a large door which was faintly outlined by dim light. There appeared to be a small hole in the door near the floor large enough for a cat to sneak through, or any other creature of similar size.

"I think I know how Dax got out," said Justin.

"I think I know how the bats got in," said Jackie.

"What's that noise?" asked Nick. "It's not more bats coming, is it?"

"I hear it, too," said Justin.

"Turn off your lights," said Jackie. "It will help us concentrate."

Justin and Nick had learned to trust Jackie's suggestions. They switched off their lights and listened. It worked.

"It's water," said Justin. "I definitely hear water."

"We're trapped," said Nick. "Do you think the water is going to make a flood in here?"

"Let's go open the door," said Jackie. She began to run and stopped just short of falling headlong into a gaping crack that ran side to side across the entire stone pathway and partially up the wall. She slowly backed away from the edge of the small chasm that had nearly swallowed her whole.

Justin and Nick joined her and pointed their lights down into the blackness.

"I can't even see the bottom," said Justin. "Dax!" he called. "Are you there, girl?" He wanted desperately to find her, but actually hoped she didn't respond from those unknown depths.

"I am sure she jumped over it," said Jackie. "Watch me." She backed up, ran and leaped effortlessly over the open crack. "See?" she said. "Easy."

Jackie's confidence gave Justin a sense of relief. "Dax probably did jump over it," he said. "I'm right behind you." He jumped and came to a sliding stop on the moist stone floor right next to her.

"I'm not leaping over that," said Nick. "I'll fall and be doomed."

"You sure are one brave pirate," taunted Jackie. "I can hear your crew now. 'Let's all follow Captain Coward into the cave for lost treasure!'"

"There's something moving on the floor behind you!" said Justin.

"Nice try," said Nick. "You guys can't trick me into jumping." He turned his own light back into the tunnel. A thick, rough-cut board lay just off to his left. "I'm going to make a bridge," he said, and bent over to pick it up.

"Come on, come on," Jackie joined Justin in urging Nick to move quickly.

"Stop trying to fool me," Nick said. The board slipped from his grasp and he felt a sharp pain in the palm of his hand. "Ouch! See what you made me do?" He tried to free both of his hands to work on removing the sliver, and struggled to hold the flashlight, using his mouth. That's when he saw it and screamed. A 3-foot northern water snake was slithering rapidly in the shadows across the floor straight at him.

Chapter Eight

Going Up?

Nick had no memory of vaulting over the crack in the tunnel floor, nor of running past Justin and Jackie. Even with a loose sneaker now missing from his foot, he was easily the first one to reach the large timber door at the end of the stone corridor.

When Jackie and Justin reached the door with him, they joined in frantically pushing against it, but in vain. The door would not budge.

Justin noticed a faint pinprick of light which revealed the presence of a keyhole in the door. "Try your skeleton key," he urged Nick.

Nick quickly grabbed at the shoelace tied around his neck and pulled at it until he exposed the key. Even though he was standing in place, he kept his feet moving. He imagined the snake slithering over his sneaker or stocking foot and wrapping around his legs. "Where did that snake come from?" he asked and fumbled to try his key in the lock. He groaned. "It's not working."

Justin dropped to his knees and grasped the door where it was broken near the floor. Now instead of

38

pushing, he tried tugging at it with both hands.

Jackie and Nick saw what he was trying to do and joined him. It was awkward and hard to get leverage, but six hands working in unison finally succeeded in pulling the door inward, even if only partially open. A blast of fresh air entered the hallway and their lungs.

Justin stuck his head and shoulders out the doorway and looked down toward the sound of the water, which was much louder now. The head lamp followed every move of his bucket hat. "It's another pit," he reported to his friends. "I can see water splashing everywhere at the bottom of it. And there are some rocks."

"Can't we get out that way?" asked Nick, and continued his strange dance, still worried about the snake. He sounded desperate.

"Meow."

Justin turned in the direction of the familiar sound. "Dax!" he cried. "How did you jump all the way over there!"

"Where is she?" asked Jackie, and leaned over Justin's back to see out the door.

"I want to see, too," said Nick. He placed the shoelace back around his neck and stuck his head under Justin's arm. The key dangled in front of his chest.

"Don't push," said Justin. "I'll fall down the pit."

Across from them on a small wooden shelf built into the wall, was Dax. Next to her was a double row of antique bottles.

Dax sat across from them on a small
wooden shelf built into the wall.

"Hey, look," said Nick. "There's one of those funny green bottles with a round bottom like the one we found in the lake with the skeleton key." He scanned the shelf. "It looks like there are keys in all the bottles!"

Jackie added her light to the scene, disorienting Dax and causing the normally sure-footed calico to misstep and nudge the round bottom bottle that was laying on its side. They all watched helplessly as it slowly rolled and then slipped off the ledge, tumbling through the air toward the water below. It missed its liquid cushion, and smashed to pieces on some jagged rocks.

"Don't move, Dax," Justin said. "We'll save you."

"Who's going to save us?" asked Nick.

Jackie continued to probe the open space in front of them with her light. "This isn't a pit," she said. "It's like an elevator shaft."

"But a lot skinnier," added Nick. "And without an elevator!"

Justin looked at Nick. "Why don't you go back and get that board? We can use it to make a bridge and Dax can walk back over to us."

Nick stared at him. "There is no way I'm going back in there with that snake," he said. "Dax is your cat. You go get the board."

"Look, there's a ladder against the wall right here next to us," said Jackie. She pointed her flashlight upward. "And there's some kind of trap door up in the ceiling above us. Come on, let's go for it." She took Justin by the shoulder, turned him, and looked

41

directly into his eyes. "If you want to get Dax, you'll just have to get on the ladder and reach back for her."

Justin felt bat wings in his stomach as he squeezed through the crack of the partially open timber door. He carefully slid his foot onto the first flat rung that was nailed to some old studs running up the wall. One wrong move and it would be down the shaft. Satisfied that his foot was fully secure, he reached up with one hand to take hold of the next rung. But before he swung himself fully onto the crude ladder, he reached back with his free hand across the open shaft for Dax. "Come on, girl," he said.

Dax moved expertly around the remaining bottles on the ledge of the shelf. She bypassed Justin's outstretched hand, however, and jumped across the open shaft directly onto his head and shoulders.

"Dax!" Justin cried. With his head lamp and bucket hat pushed down over his eyes, Justin blindly swung back for a two-handed grip on the ladder where he clung like an insect on flypaper.

"Get Dax off your head and go up the ladder, Justin," urged Jackie.

Justin didn't want to move, but slowly loosened his grip on the ladder and reached up for Dax. He eased her down and cradled her in his right arm and then began the clumsy upward climb. Every time he let go to grab a higher rung on the ladder, he felt like he was going to fall backwards.

Jackie slipped through the doorway and onto the

ladder directly below Justin. Nick closely followed, complaining about the sliver in his hand and his soggy sock that was made wet from his desperate dash across the moist stone floor.

The water splashed further and further beneath them, as straight up the dim, dank shaft they climbed, hand over hand and foot over foot, trusting the ancient wood rungs would hold all their weight.

"I'm there," Justin said, as he reached the trap door in the ceiling.

"Pop it open," said Jackie.

"I'm trying," said Justin. "It's hard to push up on it while I have Dax."

"Bang it with your head!" called an irritated Nick from somewhere beneath Jackie.

Afraid to try such an acrobatic stunt, Justin did try pressing the small trap door upward using his head and then his shoulder, but nothing would work. The door above felt like it might give way once, but without using at least one hand, he couldn't get enough power to open it. "I don't know what to do," said Justin. "We're stuck."

"You have to let go of the ladder and push on the door using your hand," Jackie instructed him. "It's the only way."

Justin sighed. He leaned his chest forward against the ladder. Facing straight ahead, he reached up with his left hand, closed his eyes and pushed with all his strength. It worked. The trap door gave way, but sprung open so suddenly that he lost his balance – *and* Dax. "No!" he cried, as he felt her slip from his right arm and begin to tumble through the air, toward the water and jagged rocks below.

Chapter Nine

A Maze Thing

Dax continued her free-fall down the open shaft, past Justin's waist, legs and feet, but not beyond Jackie's outstretched arm. "Got her!" she said, but lost her flashlight, which plummeted end-over-end and met the same fate as the falling bottle. They could all hear the familiar smash as the light hit the rocks below.

Nick was stunned. "That could have been Dax," he said. "She only has eight left."

"Eight what?" asked Jackie.

"Lives!" said Nick. "If a cat has nine lives, she definitely just used one up!"

Justin strained to look back down over his shoulder. "Thank you, Jackie!" he said.

Jackie nodded up at him. "The best way to thank me is to get us off this ladder," she said. "Let's go!"

Justin popped his head up through the hole in the ceiling. He shook his head. "You're not going to like this," he said.

"What's wrong?" asked Jackie. "More bats?"

"More snakes?" asked Nick.

"It's another tunnel," said Justin. The light from his head lamp shone down the narrow, hollow corridor, only to disappear somewhere into yet more darkness. "We won't even be able to stand up going through this one."

Still, the three explorers were glad to have the open vertical shaft behind them, and began their horizontal crawl on hands and knees through the passageway. Dax trotted slightly ahead. She turned to look back at them, and only her two unblinking eyes glowed and penetrated the darkness.

Nick was startled by Dax's eerie look. "Ouch!" he said, as he bumped his head trying to stand up and move away. "Hey, that was creepy looking." He had not liked the thought of being last in the dark, confined space and had positioned himself in the middle of the crawling, single-file line. He rubbed his head. "I don't like this at all. I feel like an ant trapped in an ant farm."

Justin ignored him and kept inching forward. There were Dax's four small footprints weaving a trail in the dust before him. He was so glad they had found her. Now they just had to find a way out of ... wherever it was they were!

At an intersection, he glanced down at the floor again and stopped. There were three possible ways to go. But there was something more disturbing than that. It looked like Dax's footprints weren't the only ones now imprinted in the dust.

Jackie was the expert on animal tracks. She squeezed

The light from Justin's head lamp shone
down the narrow, hollow corridor...

her way around Nick to join Justin again toward the front of their line.

"What do you think?" asked Justin. "Chipmunk, raccoon... rat?"

"Rats!" cried Nick. He pressed into Jackie and Justin and drew his feet under his body. "There are rats in here?" How he regretted losing his sneaker and imagined the furry vermin nipping at his poor unprotected toes. "Let me back in the middle," he said. "Let me back in the middle right now!"

"The footprints are too faint," said Jackie, as she pushed Nick off from them. "And they are all mixed up with where Dax was walking." She shook her head. "There's not enough detail for me to make them out. Just keep going."

"Which way?" asked Justin. He shined his head lamp forward again. "Left or right or straight ahead?"

"Which way did Dax go?" asked Jackie.

"I'm not sure," said Justin. "She is out of sight again, and there are tracks going in every direction."

"I vote we turn right," said Nick, who reclaimed his spot in the middle of the line.

No one argued. The three turned right, scuffing knees along the floor, sneezing from the dust, and still occasionally bumping their heads.

They turned left and then left again. The corridor was stuffy and getting stuffier.

"My knees are getting really sore," complained Nick, after their third turn. As he moved forward the skeleton key dangling from his neck moved back and forth on its string like the pendulum on a grandfather clock. "We've been trapped in here forever."

"This can't be right," said Justin, after another left turn.

"What is it?" asked Jackie.

"We've been here before," said Justin, stopping at yet another intersection. "Our scuff marks are all through the dust on the floor here."

Nick moaned. "No, no," he said. "Someone's just going to find our bones in these tunnels. We're doomed."

Justin could feel his chest tighten. He labored for breath, but it wasn't from lack of air. It was more panic. "I don't want to be in here anymore," he said. He imagined being back out on Fourth Lake, the air fresh and clean as he sailed wild and free under a wide-open blue sky.

Jackie could sense Justin's real fear. She knew what to say. "I think we should turn right this time," she said. "We haven't gone that way yet. Dax is sure to be there."

"Okay," said Justin. It had been some time since he had called out his pet's name. "Dax, can you hear me? We're coming."

There was a scratching noise coming from somewhere up ahead.

"You were right, Jackie, I think I hear her," said Justin. "Maybe she found the way out." He moved so fast, his head rocked up and down and made the lamp on top of his bucket hat act more like a strobe, as the light showing the way bounced chaotically off the low ceiling and narrow walls.

He turned another corner in pursuit of the sound, and stopped.

"What *now*?" asked Jackie, entirely frustrated she had not seen anything for the past fifteen minutes other than the bottom of a sneaker and a smelly, disgusting looking sock crawling away in front of her.

"It's a dead end," said Justin. "But it looks different, like we're going into some kind of small room." The scratching sound suddenly stopped. He moved in a little further. "There's a huge box in here." Finally, fully entering the open space with its higher ceiling and wider walls, he felt like he could breathe again.

"Let me see," said Nick, who was literally right on his heels. He sat down next to him and gasped. "That's not just a box!" he said. "That's a sea chest – a real sea chest – the kind that's filled with pirate junk and treasure!"

Jackie joined them and together they formed a small semicircle in front of the box. "No, it's not," she said. "My great-grandmother has an old trunk almost just like it. She keeps sheets and some old clothes in it."

"Let's open it," said Nick. He reached into his pocket and put his eye patch back on, which immediately produced the captain. "Give up yer treasure now," he said to the box in his pirate voice. He reached out for the lid.

There were more scratching sounds from the shadows behind the chest, and he fell back.

"Dax?" asked Justin.

"That's not Dax," said Jackie.

Three sets of beady, glowing eyes suddenly appeared on top of the box.

Somehow Nick managed to stay in character, if only for a moment. "Rotten scoundrels!" he cried. "That sea chest be ours!"

Chapter Ten

Finders Keepers?

Three furry creatures with long tails darted toward the three Adirondack kids and scurried past their exposed arms and legs out of the room and back into the maze. The squeaking of the unidentified animals as they ran was nearly drowned out by the sound of Nick's yelling and kicking.

"Quiet!" said Jackie. "They are more afraid of us than we are of them."

The pirate gathered himself and sat upright. "They were just lucky I didn't have my sword!" he spouted.

Justin slid forward and tried to open the lid on the chest. It would not move. He noticed a lock on it, and turned to Nick. "It takes a skeleton key," he said. "The key didn't work in the cave door. Maybe it will work in this."

The captain removed the key from around his neck and handed it to Justin. "I'll be watchin' yer every move," he growled. "Don't be tryin' nuthin' funny."

Jackie grabbed at Nick's eye patch. She lost her grip and the elastic band snapped it back in place.

"Hey, that hurt!" said Nick, rubbing his face and

readjusting the patch. "Why did you do that?"

"Stop talking in that stupid pirate voice," Jackie said.

Justin remained busy struggling with the stubborn lock. "The skeleton key isn't working," he said.

"Well, of course it's not," said Jackie. "What are the chances a key we found in a bottle in the lake would..."

Click.

Justin smiled.

Nick grinned, and broke into song:

"Fifteen men on the dead man's chest –"

He stopped suddenly to block another blow from Jackie.

"Talk like a pirate again and I'll be the only one singing," Jackie said, and then began her own version of the song:

"One man dead before he opened the chest –"

"Stop and help me with this," Justin said. He made room for Jackie and the pirate to join him on their knees in front of the giant trunk. "One, two, three – lift," he said.

The lid yawned stiffly open, creaking like old camp stairs. The light from Justin's lamp reflected off the contents inside, making their faces glow. They all coughed from the sudden explosive smell of moth balls.

"I told you there would only be sheets," said Jackie.

"But what's under them?" asked Nick. "Don't bother with any old seashells. Look for a bag with silver and jewels or gold or a pistol."

They removed the sheet, and there wasn't a pistol, but there was a sword that lay on top of a military uniform neatly tucked alongside some papers and a photograph of a soldier.

"Wow," said Nick. He picked up the sword, and pointed it behind them into the blackness. "I dare ye to come back now, ye scoundrels," he barked to the creatures back in the maze.

"Be careful with that," said Jackie. She looked down at the photograph. "That picture must be really old. It turned all brown."

Justin kept his head and lamp focused on the contents of the chest and probed deeper inside. Folding back the uniform revealed another sheet and underneath that sheet – "Money," he said. "There are piles of money in here."

"No way," said Nick. He lowered the sword and peered back into the chest.

"Some is green, but some of it is yellow," wondered Jackie out loud. "It's not like any money I've ever seen before."

"It's probably from another country," said Nick. He began to stuff handfuls into his pockets.

"Wait!" said Jackie. "None of this is ours. We don't even know where we are."

"Finders keepers!" argued Nick, but he knew she

was right. Slowly he began to put his fortune back into the chest.

"Shhh!" Justin whispered. "I hear voices."

"I hear them, too," said Jackie, quietly. "They're coming from inside the wall."

"I knew it," said Nick, trembling. "It's the dead captain. Just like in *Treasure Island*. He doesn't like that we found his money."

"You'd better read that book again," said Jackie.

The voices in the walls became louder, and Justin's head lamp flickered. "Oh, no," he whispered. "My battery must be going out. Get out your flashlight, Nick."

"I don't have mine," said Nick. "I lost it in the tunnel when I ran from the snake."

"I dropped mine to save Dax," said Jackie.

"Hey, where is Dax, anyway?" asked Justin. His lamp flickered again. And then again. Then they all waited helplessly as it flickered wildly and in seconds went dead.

In the pitch black, it became easier, but somehow scarier, to tell where the muffled voices were coming from.

"What are they saying?" said Nick. "What are the ghosts saying?"

"Be quiet," said Justin. "They'll hear you."

Nick yelled. "Something just touched me!" he said. "Those things are back – where's my sword!" As he groped for the weapon, he pushed into Jackie who pushed into Justin who pushed against the wall which suddenly gave way. One giant ball of arms

55

and legs tumbled and rolled together out of the darkness and into the light.

Suddenly untangled and sprawled out on a spacious hardwood floor, the three Adirondack kids were blinded and disoriented, but Justin did recognize the feel of Dax's sandpaper tongue brushing over and over against his cheek. He squinted and tried hard to focus. There were feet everywhere. In fancy shoes. But it was dead silent. He joined Jackie and Nick, who were already sitting up and rubbing their eyes. The palms of their hands, covered with dust and dried mud, painted their eye sockets black.

Looking like the big losers in a boxing match, they gazed up from the floor and realized they were seated in the midst of a large group of adults, all dressed up in formal gowns and tuxedos, who were frozen in place and just staring down at them.

A young boy, also in a tuxedo, stepped out from behind one of the adults. His familiar voice finally broke the silence. "Justin? Jackie? Nick?...Dax? How did you get in here?" It was Douglas.

Chapter Eleven

Secret of the Skeleton Key

"I smell chicken," said Nick.

"It's not chicken," said Douglas. "We were just about to sit down and eat some stuffed Cornish hen."

"It's kind of weird seeing you in that tuxedo," said Justin.

"It still smells like chicken," insisted Nick.

Several of the adults had the small section of the dining room wall propped open where the kids had entered the room.

Nick was amused, watching two of the grown-ups crouching and kneeling in funny positions while trying to slide the heavy chest into the room without getting their fancy clothes all dirty. "There's no way you're going to stay clean in there," he said.

"This is the boathouse?" said Jackie, amazed. "It's more like a real house in here."

"It *is* a real house," said Douglas. "Instead of like a house with a garage for cars, there are a bunch of boat slips underneath us."

"That's not the only difference," said Mr. Taylor,

holding something he had removed from the open chest. "Unlike most houses, this one apparently has secret passages in all the walls. Come and take a look at this."

Dinner was on hold as hosts and guests moved the special china on the dining room table aside to make space for the unrolling of a large scroll.

"We never even saw that in there," said Justin.

"It's a treasure map, isn't it?" said Nick. "Look for some writing in red ink, or a place called Skeleton Island!" He raised the sword, making everyone gasp. From the looks on their faces, he figured it was time to set the saber down on the table. Justin and Jackie were relieved.

"It is not a map," said Mr. Taylor. "It's a hand-drawn blueprint of the boathouse from when it was built in 1902. It appears there is an entire series of narrow passageways hidden in the walls here. If these plans are accurate, it looks like there are small trap doors that open into almost every room in the house."

"What about the sword and the uniform and all the funny-looking money?" asked Justin.

An older, distinguished-looking gentleman with gray hair and a beard removed his glasses and cleared his throat. "This chest holds a wealth of American history," he began. "All are artifacts from the Civil War. And judging from the papers and photograph, I am thinking there is a good chance these items are connected with the Adirondack

58

118th infantry regiment that was mustered out of Plattsburgh in August of 1862."

"There was definitely not any mustard anywhere in that chest," said Nick. "Unless maybe the rats got it."

"Rats?" asked a tall woman standing next to him wearing pink lipstick, a pink dress, pink hat and pink shoes. There was a look of terror in her eyes. "There are rats?" she asked again, as even her cheeks flushed pink. She called out to anyone who would listen and pointed toward the open chest with her long pink fingernails. "Has anyone seen rats?"

Jackie quickly pulled Nick away from the frightened lady. "Not mustard," she whispered. "Mustered. They mustered the soldiers. It sort of means they got men signed up to be in the army."

"This is amazing," said Mr. Taylor, who continued to study the blueprint and describe his discoveries out loud. His finger followed a series of tunnels and stopped. "Look at this. It appears there is a false wall behind the boat slips that leads straight up into the main house."

The Adirondack kids looked at each other.

Justin looked over Mr. Taylor's shoulder at the blueprints. "We were in there!" he said.

"We were looking for Dax who was lost in the cave," said Jackie, pointing to the calico cat who stood staring at the dining room table toward the quickly cooling Cornish hens.

"Yes," said Nick. "And we finally found her on a shelf in the elevator shaft with a ton of old bottles."

Everyone stood or sat while sipping on sodas and listened with fascination as Justin, Jackie and Nick took turns explaining how the lost arrow led them to the hole in the ground, through the cave that really wasn't a cave, up the open shaft and finally through the maze of tunnels to the old chest and into the dining room.

Of course, Nick's parts of the story were slightly exaggerated, as he described his heroic fights with "vampire bats," a "snake that was nearly 10 feet long" and "tunnels filled with dozens of hungry rats," which made the lady in pink nearly faint. In fact, his version of the story made everyone a little uncomfortable.

"Tell me more about the bottles," said Mr. Taylor.

"Well, it was hard to see, but it looked like most of the bottles might have had more keys in them," said Justin.

"And there were labels on some of the bottles," offered Jackie. "I think I remember reading the word, *Saratoga*, on at least one of them."

"One of the bottles with a round bottom rolled off the shelf," said Nick. "It missed the water and smashed on some rocks."

While Nick was talking, two men shifted the chest to set it against the wall, and the skeleton key dropped out of the lock and clattered across the wood floor.

Justin picked it up. "The bottle that fell looked just like the one we found in the lake with this skeleton key in it," he said. "And that's how we opened the chest and found all the Civil War stuff."

"So the camp and the chest finally gave up their secrets after all these years," said Mr. Taylor with a satisfied laugh.

The Adirondack kids looked puzzled.

"The bottle you found with the skeleton key that opened the chest must have rolled off that shelf during the earthquake," Mr. Taylor explained. "I'm actually surprised the vibration from that tremor didn't cause all of the them to fall. Your bottle missed the rocks, hit the water and was carried out by the waves under the boathouse and into the lake."

Nick had inched his way toward the food at the far end of the table and began peeking underneath the silver tray covers.

"Part of Route 28 near Eagle Bay broke completely apart this morning," said one of the dinner guests. "The earthquake may have shaken open the old buried entrance you discovered, and made that deep crack in the stone floor as well."

Mr. Taylor shook his head in agreement. "But that doesn't explain why the corridor from the boat-house to the forest was even made over a hundred years ago in the first place," he said. "It's not even on these blueprints. Maybe we'll never know."

Justin held up the key. "There are a lot more bot-tles and skeleton keys," he said. "Maybe you'll find the answer to that secret with another one of these."

"Excuse me," interrupted Nick, with a silver tray cover in his hand. "Do you think it would be all right if we had some of this chicken?"

Chapter Twelve

The Anything That Floats Race

"Be prepared to lose, sea dogs!" barked Nick, with eye patch on and sword held high from atop the cabin of the *Robert Louis Stevenson*. He began to sing as he hoisted the black Jolly Roger flag with its skull and crossbones high above the mast that held a single-sheet sail:

"Fifteen men on the dead man's chest – "

Justin and Dax rounded out the crew on the sinister ship that had been towed into place at the contest starting line.

Fourth Lake was never more blue. And never more perfect for sailing was the breeze that blew.

A host of kayaks, guide boats, rafts and canoes dotted and drifted all along the starting line that stretched between two large, orange buoys on the north side of Cedar Island. The main requirement for entry? Any vessel entered into the race was to be powered by sail.

Jackie ignored Nick's taunting. She was captain

of her own boat now, and was all business. She sat aboard her classic Sunfish with triangular blue, red, orange and yellow sail, all ready to race across the water surface to victory with her sole shipmate, Douglas. The colorful sail draped loosely on the mast and luffed in the easy breeze. Jackie kept her eye on her watch, and waited for the sound of the starting gun.

A scratchy voice sounded across the lake through a powerful bullhorn from the deck of the official committee boat. "Welcome, ladies and gentlemen, to the First Annual Anything That Floats Race," said Mr. Charles Marke, his words piercing both air and eardrums. "What a lovely day we have for the race. And we expect you all will follow the rules of safety and fairness."

In contrast to his obnoxious voice, Mr. Marke was all dressed in pressed white pants and a finely fitted navy blue jacket trimmed with gold.

He stopped briefly and took hold of the black brim of his otherwise bright white captain's cap to save it from blowing away. "We would like to thank all of the following people for making this event possible," he continued, his penetrating voice punishing the sailors, the spectators and even the seagulls which temporarily flew for the island and distant shoreline.

Nick called from his perch down to Justin on the deck. "Can you even hear what he is saying?" he asked.

"Welcome to the first annual
Anything That Floats Race," said Mr. Marke.

Justin shook his head back and forth. "I have no idea," he said. "But he sure is annoying."

It seemed the people on the committee boat were suffering the most. As Mr. Marke droned on and on with announcement after announcement, you could see them covering their ears and inching as far away from him as they could without falling overboard. He was still talking, when someone else on the boat finally shot the starting gun and the boats were off.

Sails could be heard popping and snapping as they were hoisted by young sailors all along the starting line and were slapped and filled by the wind.

Justin had his eyes on Jackie and Douglas. It didn't matter to him if he and Nick won the race, just so long as they beat the two of them.

Captain Flint and his mate were still attempting to raise their own sail, when Jackie's vessel cut in front of the *Robert Louis Stevenson* and began to head for the committee boat. She appeared to have the Sunfish headed in the wrong direction.

"Hey, what's going on?" said Nick. "They're in our way."

Justin admitted the move looked strange, but he knew Jackie always had a plan. "What are you doing?" he called out to the Sunfish.

"I'm tacking," said Jackie.

Nick let go of the sail. "Did she say she is attacking?" he asked, and sprang into action. "Man the cannons! We'll attack first!"

Before Justin could suggest that tacking might be

some kind of sailing term, Nick had secured an armful of water balloons from inside the cabin and was loading one of them into the wide elastic band of his gigantic man-sized slingshot that was bolted on the rail toward the back of the boat. "Fire!" he said, as he pulled the elastic band taut, and let go. The balloon took off like a rocket and flew over Jackie's rainbow sail, falling harmlessly near the committee boat.

The bullhorn blasted. "You there – in the pirate boat – that will be quite enough," bellowed Mr. Marke. Then he turned on his own helpers and snapped some orders through the horn.

Jackie was picking up speed and Nick loaded more ammunition. "Fire!" he cried and a second water balloon sprang through the air and over the Sunfish. This time the balloon made contact, breaking and splashing against the hull of the committee boat.

"Stop it, Nick," said Justin. "I don't want to be kicked out of the race. Forget the fight and raise the sail. Everyone's going to beat us."

Nick wasn't listening. Jackie's sail was now full of wind and he knew it would soon be out of range permanently. "Fire!" he said.

Mr. Marke had given his last warning and stood to officially disqualify the *Robert Louis Stevenson* from the race. "I am sorry. According to Rule Number Eight, your boat is –"

He never got out another word as the third balloon reached him and entered the end of his raised bullhorn. Caught more by surprise than by force, the sudden explosion of water sent the bullhorn in one direction, the bright white cap in another direction, and Mr. Marke in his trim navy jacket and pressed pants stumbling off the back side of the boat and into Fourth Lake.

Justin wasn't sure, but he thought he saw people on the committee boat clapping. There was a tap on his shoulder. It was the tip of Nick's sword. "What are you doing?" he asked.

"Where were ye during the battle?" Nick asked firmly, squinting through his single patchless eye. "Get ye on the plank now, ye traitor."

"Meow."

Nick turned. Dax was already on the long, wide board that was nailed to the bow of the boat and extended out over the water.

"So that's how ye want it," said Nick. "Fine, ye can go to the sharks first!" He moved out onto the board and poked his sword toward Dax. "Walk the plank," he said. "With less weight on the boat, it will be easier to catch up with the others!"

"Leave her alone," said Justin.

"Quiet," said Nick. "There will be no mutiny on my ship." Dax inched away from him toward the end of the plank. As Nick closed in on her, she looked side to side down at the water. There was no more room to move.

"I mean it, Nick," warned Justin. "Leave Dax alone or –"

There was a sudden cracking sound where the plank was nailed to the boat. Nick looked back over his shoulder to investigate, and Dax made her move. Darting between his feet, she was back on the deck when the board snapped, taking the stunned and mouthy captain with it into the sea.

While Nick clung to the plank floating in the lake and was spitting out water, Justin looked out at the horizon, and sighed. There was a fleet of small boats with billowed sails all clustered together. But far, far ahead of them all, a single sailboat was already rounding the distant buoy to head back for the finish line. It was a Sunfish with a blue, red, orange and yellow sail.

epilogue

It looked and smelled like rain.

The race was just yesterday, but already it seemed to Justin like it was a long time ago. He sat in his wicker chair on the sleeping porch overlooking Fourth Lake, holding his first sailing trophy. He and Nick had won the top prize for, *The Most Unusual Boat.*

Of course, the top trophy went to Jackie and Douglas for crossing the finish line first. He was just relieved there was not a *Good-Try-Even-Though-You-Came-In-Last-Place* trophy. Nick had said he felt so badly the *Robert Louis Stevenson* had not even moved an inch in the race, that Justin could keep their trophy at his camp first.

They had heard Mr. Marke didn't want to give them a trophy at all, and even wanted to ban them from the next year's race and every race after that for the rest of their lives. But it seemed many of the adults were actually quite happy Mr. Marke had stopped using the bullhorn. They came to their rescue and convinced Mr. Marke that the water balloons were all just good fun and that no harm was intended.

Getting the boat ready to race had been fun. And so were the cave and lost tunnels, except for the bats and rats. It still amazed him that families had lived in the boathouse for years and not known the secrets hidden there.

He and Jackie and Nick had been right. The bottles on the shelf did have more keys in them. How many other secrets did the old boathouse have? What secrets were in their own camp? Or in Nick's? Or Jackie's? He wondered if every old camp in the Adirondacks had secret passageways and hidden chests just waiting to be discovered and opened.

It started to rain.

Justin stood and placed the trophy on his dresser. He picked up the copy of *Treasure Island* he borrowed from Nick, who had not let it go easily. It was hard to believe Nick had read *Treasure Island* two times already that summer. He didn't think Nick hardly read anything at all! What secrets did that story hold? What hold did that story have on Nick? He decided to see for himself and returned with it to the wicker chair. He opened the book. "Part One," he whispered. "The Old Buccaneer..."

It began to rain harder.

Robert Louis Stevenson wrote the classic adventure story, *Treasure Island*. Published in 1883, it was his first novel. The famous author lived and wrote one winter in Saranac Lake, New York. *Photograph © Robert Louis Stevenson Memorial Cottage, Saranac Lake, NY. Used by permission.*

DAX FACTS

Robert Louis Stevenson was the author of the classic book, *Treasure Island*.

It is believed Stevenson wrote the adventure having been inspired by his stepson, Lloyd Osbourn, who asked him to write a story and who had even drawn a treasure map with places named on it, like Skeleton Island. The two were very close, and later in life, stepfather and stepson would even write together.

Born in England in 1850, Robert Louis Stevenson traveled to Switzerland, France and the Island of Samoa.

But it was during the winter of 1887–1888, when the world-famous author lived and worked six months at Baker Cottage in Saranac Lake, New York.

The cottage where Stevenson lived is still there in the Adirondack community on Stevenson Lane, and is now a museum which holds the largest collection of Stevenson personal artifacts in America. Even the pieces of furniture in one of the rooms are those which he and his family members used more than 100 years ago, including a desk and chair where the author sat and wrote.

Robert Louis Stevenson died in the Samoan Islands in 1894, when he was just 44 years old. Among his most famous stories along with *Treasure Island* were *Kidnapped* and *Dr. Jeckyl and Mr. Hyde.*

The historic Robert Louis Stevenson Cottage and Museum in Saranac Lake, New York, holds the largest collection of Stevenson personal artifacts in America. Visit the museum's website at www.Pennypiper.org. *Photograph by Gary VanRiper © 2006 Adirondack Kids Press*

Opposite: Thousands of bottles are on display at the National Bottle Museum in Ballston Spa, New York. The museum helps preserve the history of bottle making. Visit the National Bottle Museum at www.nationalbottlemuseum.org

🐾 DAX FACTS

Did you now there is a museum for bottles? There is!
Located in the heart of the Village of Ballston
Spa, New York, the **National Bottle Museum**
has helped preserve the history of the nation's first
major industry – bottle making. One entire wall of
the museum's first floor features shelves with nearly
2000 bottles of various colors, shapes and forms.

The bottle which Justin Robert pulls out of Fourth
Lake in *The Adirondack Kids #6 – Secret of the
Skeleton Key*, is known as an "egg" bottle which
features a round bottom in the shape of an egg. The
invention of the round bottom forced those storing
the bottles to lay them on their sides. That helped the
corks stay evenly wet from the inside liquids and
ensure a safe seal! The bottles could also travel on
tossing ships and roll around without breaking.

DAX FACTS

The **Pileated Woodpecker** is the largest woodpecker in the Adirondacks. The largely black bird with a white throat and some white accent on its head, throat and wings is nearly a foot and a half long and sports a large red crest. The bird makes large rectangular or oval holes in dead trees in search of insects. Its powerful bill can easily chisel wood chips from three to six inches long!

Pileated Woodpecker. *Photograph © 2004 by Eric Dresser (www.nbnp.com)*

About the Authors

Gary and Justin VanRiper (*see photo on opposite page*) are a father-and-son writing team residing in Camden, New York, with their family and cat, Dax. They spend many summer and autumn days at camp on Fourth Lake in the Adirondacks.

The Adirondack Kids® began as a short home writing exercise when Justin was in third grade. Encouraged after a public reading of an early draft at a Parents As Reading Partners (PARP) program in their school district, the project grew into a middle reader chapter book series.

About the Illustrators

Carol McCurn VanRiper lives and works in Camden, New York. She is also the wife and mother, respectively, of *The Adirondack Kids*® co-authors, Gary and Justin VanRiper. She inherited the job as publicist when *The Adirondack Kids*® progressed from a family dream into a small company.

Susan Loeffler is a freelance illustrator who lives and works in Upstate, New York.

Gary and Justin VanRiper at the Robert Louis Stevenson Cottage and Museum in Saranac Lake, New York.
Photograph by Carol VanRiper © 2006 Adirondack Kids Press

The Adirondack Kids® #1

Justin Robert is ten years old and likes computers, biking and peanut butter cups. But his passion is animals. When an uncommon pair of Common Loons takes up residence on Fourth Lake near the family camp, he will do anything he can to protect them.

The Adirondack Kids® #2
Rescue on Bald Mountain

Justin Robert and Jackie Salsberry are on a special mission. It is Fourth of July weekend in the Adiron-dacks and time for the annual ping-pong ball drop at Inlet. Their best friend, Nick Barnes, has won the opportunity to release the balls from a seaplane, but there is just one problem. He is afraid of heights. With a single day remaining before the big event, Justin and Jackie decide there is only one way to help Nick overcome his fear. Climb Bald Mountain!

All on sale wherever great books on the Adirondacks are found.

The **Adirondack Kids**® #3
The Lost Lighthouse

Justin Robert, Jackie Salsberry and Nick Barnes are fishing under sunny Adirondack skies when a sudden and violent storm chases them off Fourth Lake and into an unfamiliar forest – a forest that has harbored a secret for more than 100 years.

The **Adirondack Kids**® #4
The Great Train Robbery

It's all aboard the train at the North Creek station, and word is out there are bandits in the region. Will the train be robbed? Justin Robert and Jackie Salsberry are excited. Nick Barnes is bored – but he won't be for long.

Also available on **The Adirondack Kids**® official web site
www.ADIRONDACKKIDS.com
Watch for more adventures of The Adirondack Kids® coming soon.

The Adirondack Kids® #5
Islands in the Sky

Justin Robert, Jackie Salsberry and Nick Barnes head for the Adirondack high peaks wilderness – while Justin's calico cat, Dax, embarks on an unexpected tour of the Adirondack Park.

The Adirondack Kids® #6
Secret of the Skeleton Key

While preparing their pirate ship for the Anything That Floats Race, Justin and Nick discover an antique bottle riding the waves on Fourth Lake. Inside the bottle is a key that leads The Adirondack Kids to unlock an old camp mystery.

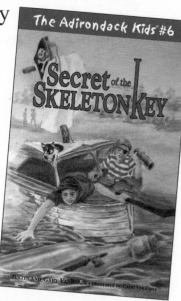

Over **60,000** Adirondack Kids Books in Print!

All on sale wherever great books on the Adirondacks are found.

The **Adirondack Kids®** Story & Coloring Book
Runaway Dax

Artist Susan Loeffler brings a favorite Adirondack Kids® character – Dax – to life in 32 coloring book illustrations set to a storyline for young readers written by Adirondack Kids® co-creator and author, Justin VanRiper.

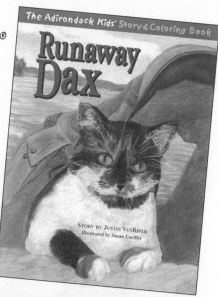

The **Adirondack Kids® Wall Poster**

17" x 22" – Full Color
Features Justin, Nick, Jackie and Dax in the Adirondack Mountains. Also featured are a black bear, pileated woodpecker and red admiral butterflies, all creatures of the Adirondacks.

Also available on **The Adirondack Kids®** official web site
www.ADIRONDACKKIDS.com
Watch for more adventures of The Adirondack Kids® coming soon.

*Watch for more adventures
of The Adirondack Kids® coming soon.*